TAXI! TAXI!

by Cari Best
Illustrated by Dale Gottlieb

Little, Brown and Company
BOSTON   NEW YORK   TORONTO   LONDON

For Alexandra, Peter, and David
and especially for Poops
— C. B.

For Uncle Sammy
— D. G.

Please note that Tina's name for her father is pronounced "poppy."

Text copyright © 1994 by Cari Best
Illustrations copyright © 1994 by Dale Gottlieb

First Edition

Library of Congress Cataloging-in-Publication Data

Best, Cari.
   Taxi! Taxi! / by Cari Best ; illustrated by Dale Gottlieb. — 1st
ed.
   p.   cm.
   Summary: Tina spends each Sunday with her father, a taxicab driver.
   ISBN 0-316-09259-2
   (1. Fathers and daughters — Fiction. 2. Taxicabs — Fiction.
3. City and town life — Fiction.)   I. Gottlieb, Dale, 1952– ill.
II. Title.
PZ7.B46575Tax 1994
(E) — dc20   92-32249

10 9 8 7 6 5 4 3 2 1

SC

Published simultaneously in Canada
by Little, Brown & Company (Canada) Limited

Printed in Hong Kong

The illustrations in this book were done in oil pastels on hot-pressed Fabriano Artistico paper that is 100 percent cotton and acid free. The pastels were then rubbed with mineral spirits on cotton.
Color separations by South China Printing Company.
Text set in Barcelona at Typographic House.
Printed and bound by South China Printing Company.

Today is Sunday. The sun pours from the sky like milk from a pitcher.

It shines on Mr. Henry's motorcycle.

And on Mrs. Sweeney's happy flowers.

There is Mr. Morelli cleaning his paintbrushes.

And Anita helping her mother hang the baby's diapers out to dry.

The purple flags outside Mr. Salazar's fruit-and-vegetable
store dance and sparkle.
And so does Tina, who is waiting for her *papi*.

Papi drives a shiny yellow taxi all over the big city. He doesn't live with Tina and her mama. He lives someplace else. But on Sundays, Papi switches on his taxi's OFF DUTY light. No work today! And he comes to see Tina.

Tina has waited all week for Sunday to come. At twelve o'clock sharp, she puts on her Sunday hat and her Sunday smile. She takes the picture she painted just for Papi and goes downstairs.

While she waits, Tina counts red cars. *Uno, dos, tres, cuatro, cinco . . . seis.*
Fire trucks don't count! But no Papi yet.

Then she sings a little song:

> T my name is Tina,
> And my *papi*'s name is Tony.
> We come from the city,
> And we sell . . .
> Taxis!

Tina laughs, but still no Papi.
So she finds a crack in the sidewalk and jumps backward and forward and sideways over it. A few yellow taxis go zooming by. But not Papi's yellow taxi. He has the shiniest yellow taxi in the whole city.

Just then, Anita walks past with her mother and the baby.
"I'm waiting for my *papi*," says Tina.
"Have a nice time!" says Anita's mother.
"See you later," says Anita.

Mr. Morelli rides by on his bicycle with his dog, Bruno, close behind.

"I have my painting for my *papi*," says Tina.

"Lovely," says Mr. Morelli. "Come paint with me again soon!"

Some Sundays, Tina waits and waits. And dances and counts. And sings and jumps. But Papi doesn't come.

"He must be busy," says Mama, "driving people around the city."
"But Sunday is his day off," says Tina. "Did Papi forget?"
Tina always remembers.
She crosses her fingers on both hands and hopes Papi won't forget today.

Then, just as she starts to count airplanes, the shiniest yellow taxi in the city slows down right in front of her.
Tina claps her hands when she sees Papi, and remembers their special game.
"Taxi! Taxi!" she calls, waving her arms.
Papi pulls his taxi over to the curb and jumps out.

"At your service, *señorita*," he says with a bow. *"¡Qué bonita!"* What a pretty painting! He hangs Tina's picture next to the ivy plant in his taxi.

Then Papi toots the horn to tell Mama they are leaving — and off they go!

Past Mrs. Sweeney's apartment, with the orange curtains, and the happy flowers on the fire escape.

Past the painted palm trees under Mr. Morelli's window.

Past the library, where Tina and Anita go after school.

And the Laundromat, with
the flashing neon letters.

Past the grocery store. And
the purple banners around
Mr. Salazar's sign, which
says SIEMPRE LO MEJOR.
Always the best.

Good-bye, playground with
the climb-on dinosaur.
And the parked cars that
don't work anymore.
Past the empty lots with
every kind of color in them.
And all the other yellow taxis
that will stay in the city today.

Papi's taxi goes up one road and down another. So many roads, going crisscross like a pretzel.
"Where are *we* going today?" Tina asks.
"It's a surprise," says Papi. Like he says every Sunday.
Well, almost every Sunday.

Tina and Papi drive and drive. There is nothing but blue
and green.
Suddenly Papi stops. "Here we are!" he says.
"Listen to the air," says Tina. "It's so quiet."
"Not for long," says Papi, who knows how noisy farms
can get.

They walk down a road made of dirt. There are flowers
everywhere. Papi knows all their names — buttercup,
Queen Anne's lace, black-eyed Susan — and soon Tina does,
too. Tina thinks Papi must know everything.

They eat lunch near a pond. Tina takes a big bite out of a sweet, juicy tomato. Papi grew it himself.
Some squawking birds help them finish, and three ducks nibble right out of Tina's hand. "Aiee! It tickles."

Then Tina and Papi visit the pigs. Papi makes hungry pig noises. "How do you do it, Papi?" Tina asks, trying hard to copy the sounds, like hiccups.

So Papi shows Tina, and soon they are both oinking and hiccuping and laughing.

"You're so silly, Papi." Tina giggles.

When they pass a man selling balloons, Papi buys one.
"For my best girl," he says, presenting it to Tina. "*Para mi
chica la más preciosa.*"
Tina squeezes Papi's big hand. "I love you so-o-o much,"
she says. "This is the *best* Sunday ever. I wish you lived with
me and Mama. Then I could see you every day."

Papi smiles a sad smile and gives Tina a hug. "I love you, too," he says, "even when I'm not with you." He lifts her up on his shoulders, and soon they gallop away like a cowgirl on a horse, leaving clouds of dust behind them. After a while, Papi looks at his watch and helps Tina down.

"It's getting late, *querida,* and tonight I have to work. But just one more minute!" he says, pointing to a small green plant with yellow flowers. "Now you can grow tomatoes just like I do. Whenever you feel lonely, talk to him. And don't forget the water!"

"Do *you* talk to your plants when you're lonely?" Tina asks.

"*Por supuesto.*" Of course. "All the time. And always about you."

Now they must hurry back to Papi's taxi. On the way, they pass a family with a mama, a *papi,* and a little girl. I have two families, Tina thinks. Papi and me. And Mama and me.

In no time at all, Papi's shiny yellow taxi goes up one road and down another. Onto one highway and then onto the next. Soon the blue and green are gone and the colors of the city are back again. Tina begins to see other yellow taxis. And empty lots with every kind of color in them.
The sounds of the country are far away. Listen to the air now!

There is the playground with
the climb-on dinosaur.
And there is Anita right
on top. *"¡Hola, Anita!"*

And the grocery store.
Mr. Henry is just coming out.
He is carrying a big brown
bag. Tina waves, and Papi
pulls over.
"Taxi, Mr. Henry?" Papi asks.
Mr. Henry climbs in, holding
the bag of groceries on his lap.

GROCE

IN   C

One block farther and Mrs. Sweeney is leaving the Laundromat with a load of clean clothes in her basket. The neon sign flashes ABIERTO. Open. "Taxi, Mrs. Sweeney?" asks Papi. Mrs. Sweeney climbs in, too. Tina can hardly see her face behind the big basket.

Down the street, Mr. Salazar has just closed his fruit-and-vegetable store for the day. "*¡Siempre lo mejor!*" he says to his last customer, just as Papi and Tina pull up. "Taxi, Señor Salazar?" And Mr. Salazar smiles and climbs in, too.

On the next corner, Papi stops his taxi for a red light. Anita and her mother and the baby are coming back from the playground. "Taxi, Anita?" asks Papi.
Mr. Henry, Mrs. Sweeney, and Mr. Salazar take a deep breath. They all squeeze together, and in climb Anita, her mother, and the baby.
Tina and Anita giggle.

Just when Papi's shiny yellow taxi has all the passengers it can hold, who should Tina see but Mr. Morelli and Bruno. Papi winks at Tina. This time, she gets to ask:

"Taxi, Mr. Morelli? There is just one more seat, right next to me!"

"Lovely," says Mr. Morelli, with Bruno on his lap.

"You have *some papi*," declares Mr. Henry to Tina.
"You have *some papi*," echoes Mrs. Sweeney. Then Mr. Salazar,
Anita, her mother, and Mr. Morelli chime in, too: "You have *some papi!*"
"I know," says Tina proudly. "I have the best *papi* in the world."

This Sunday is almost over. There is no more sun left in the sky. And now there are no more passengers in Papi's taxi. Tina switches off the light in the OFF DUTY sign. Papi pulls his taxi over to the curb and jumps out. It is time for Tina and Papi to play their special game.

"*Adiós, señorita mía,*" he says, tipping his hat.

"*Adiós, Papi,*" Tina says, giving him a big kiss. "Soon we'll have *my* tomatoes for our picnics!"

Tina watches as Papi's taxi drives slowly away.
Then she sings:

T my name is Tina,
And my *papi's* name is Tony.
We come from the city,
And we sell ...
Tomatoes!

Tina smiles. "*Vamos,* little tomato plant. Let's go upstairs.
Mama is waiting."